Ladybird Readers

The Elves and the Shoemaker

Series Editor: Sorrel Pitts
Text adapted by Sorrel Pitts
Illustrated by Virginia Allyn

LADYBIRD BOOKS

UK | USA | Canada | Ireland | Australia
India | New Zealand | South Africa

Ladybird Books is part of the Penguin Random House group of companies
whose addresses can be found at global.penguinrandomhouse.com.
www.penguin.co.uk   www.puffin.co.uk   www.ladybird.com

Penguin
Random House.
UK

First published 2016
003

Copyright © Ladybird Books Ltd, 2016

The moral rights of the author and illustrator have been asserted.

Printed in China

A CIP catalogue record for this book is available from the British Library

ISBN: 978-0-241-25385-4

Ladybird Readers

The Elves and the Shoemaker

Picture words

shoemaker

shoemaker's wife

rich woman

rich man

cut

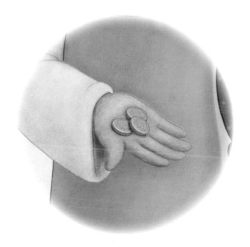

gold coins

elves

leather

In the past, there lived a poor shoemaker and his wife.

"This is all the leather I've got now," said the shoemaker. "I can make only one more pair of shoes."

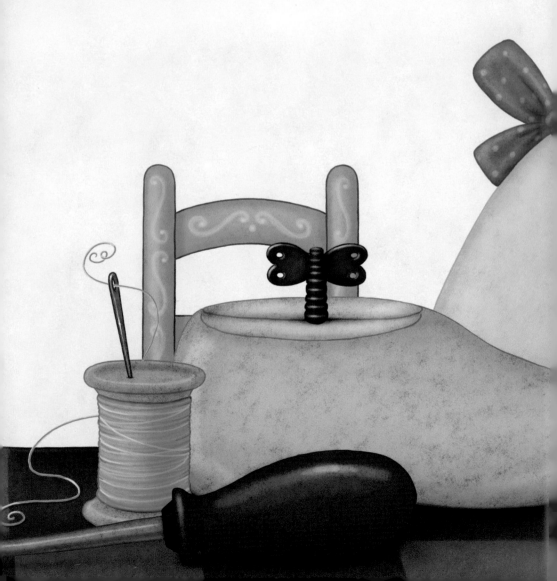

That night, the shoemaker
cut the leather.

"I can make these shoes in
the morning," he said. He left
the leather in the shop and
he went to bed.

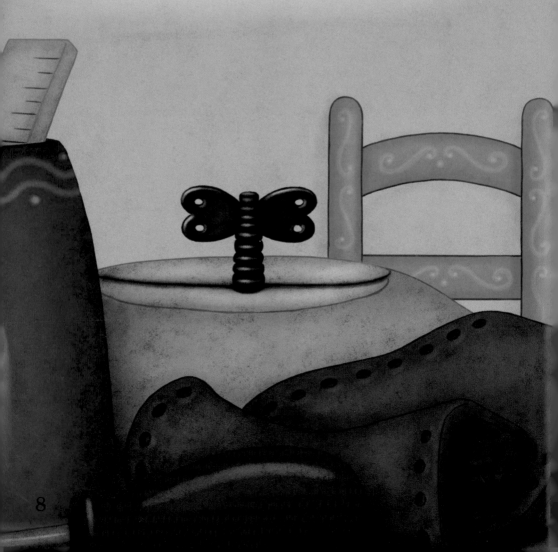

In the morning, the shoemaker came downstairs. He was very surprised because the leather was now a pair of beautiful shoes.

The shoemaker called his wife.
"Did you make these shoes?"
he said.

"No," said his wife. "I didn't
make those shoes!"

Then, a rich woman came into the shop and she saw the shoes. "These are the most beautiful shoes in the world," she said.

And she gave the shoemaker three gold coins.

The shoemaker used the coins to buy more leather.

That night, he cut the leather and he left it on the table. Then he went to bed.

In the morning, there were
two pairs of beautiful shoes
on the table.

The shoemaker called his wife.
"Did you make these shoes?"
he said.

"No," said his wife. "I didn't
make those shoes!"

Then, a rich man came into the shop. "What beautiful shoes!" he said. "I must buy them. Please take these six gold coins."

The shoemaker bought
more leather with the coins.
"Now, I can make three pairs
of shoes," he said.

That night, he cut the leather
and he left it on the table.
Then, he went to bed.

The next morning, the shoemaker
came downstairs.

On the table were three pairs
of beautiful shoes.

The shoemaker called his wife.
"We must find the person who is
making these beautiful shoes,"
he said.

The shoemaker worked hard. He cut the leather for four pairs of shoes. But that night the shoemaker and his wife didn't go to bed. They waited and watched.

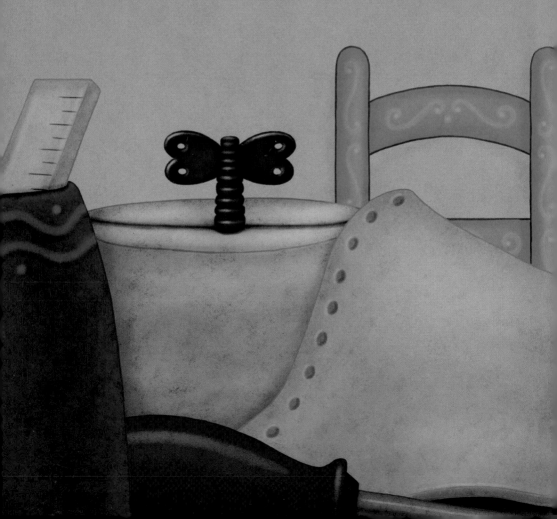

At twelve o'clock, the door
opened. Two little elves in
old clothes came into the
shop. They jumped on the
table and opened their little,
green bags.

The elves worked all night.
In the morning, there were
four pairs of beautiful shoes.
Then, they took their bags
and left the shop.

The shoemaker said to his wife,
"The elves are helping us, but
how can we help them?"

"I know!" said his wife.

The shoemaker and his wife worked very hard. They made two pairs of little green shoes and some little green clothes. Then, they made two little green hats.

That night, they left the little green shoes, hats, and clothes in the shop. Then, they waited for the elves.

At twelve o'clock, the door of the shop opened and the elves came in.

When they saw the little, green shoes, the little, green clothes, and the little, green hats, the elves were very surprised. They liked their new clothes very much.

The little elves came every night to help the shoemaker and his wife. They made many beautiful shoes. And the shoemaker and his wife made lots of little clothes for the elves.

The shoemaker and his wife,
and the two little elves all
lived happily for many years.

Activities

The key below describes the skills practiced in each activity.

Spelling and writing

Reading

Speaking

Critical thinking

Preparation for the Cambridge Young Learners Exams

1 **Look and read. Choose the correct words and write them on the lines.** 📖 ✏️ ❁

elves   gold coins   cut   shoemaker

1 This is a person who makes shoes.

shoemaker

2 We do this to make a thing smaller.

....

3 We buy things with these.

....

4 These are very small people in stories who like to help other people.

....

2 Look and read.
Write yes or no. 📖 ✏️ ⭐

In the past, there lived a poor shoemaker and his wife.

"This is all the leather I've got now," said the shoemaker. "I can make only one more pair of shoes."

1 The shoemaker lived
with his wife.   ......yes......

2 The shoemaker and his
wife were rich.   ....

3 The shoemaker needed
more leather.   ....

4 The shoemaker could
only make two more
pairs of shoes.   ....

3 **Look and read. Choose the correct words and write them on the lines.** 📖 ✏️ ⬡

wife   surprised   rich   shoes   leather

1 In the morning, the shoemaker did

not find his ___leather___ .

2 He found a pair of _____ .

3 He was very _____ .

4 He called to his _____ ,

"Did you make these shoes?"

5 Then, a _____ woman

came into the shop.

4 **Work with a friend.**
Talk about the two pictures.
How are they different? 🗨

a    b

Example:

> *In picture a, the shoemaker is not happy.*

> *In picture b, the shoemaker is happy.*

5 Look and read. Write yes or no. 📖 ✏️ ⬡

Then, a rich woman came into the shop and she saw the shoes. "These are the most beautiful shoes in the world," she said.

And she gave the shoemaker three gold coins.

1 A poor woman came into the shop.   no

2 She loved the shoes.

3 "These are the ugliest shoes in the world," she said.

4 She gave the shoemaker five gold coins.

6 **Work with a friend.**
Talk about the two pictures.
How are they different? 🗨

a

Then, a rich woman came into
the shop and she saw the shoes.
"These are the most beautiful
shoes in the world," she said.

And she gave the shoemaker
three gold coins.

14

b

Then, a rich man came into the
shop. "What beautiful shoes!"
he said. "I must buy them.
Please take these six gold coins."

20

Example:

In picture a, there
is a rich woman.

In picture b,
there is a rich man.

7 Read the text. Choose the correct words and write them on the lines. 📖 ✏️ ✦

1 How	What	Who
2 must	must to	has to
3 to take	took	take
4 buy	bought	made

Then, a rich man came into the shop.

"¹ _____What_____ beautiful shoes!"

he said. "I ² _____ buy them.

Please ³ _____ these six

gold coins." The shoemaker

⁴ _____ more leather with

the coins.

Circle the correct word.

The next night, the shoemaker worked very hard. He cut the leather for four pairs of shoes. But this time, the shoemaker and his wife hid in the shop.

1 The next morning, the shoemaker **come** / (**came**) downstairs.

2 "We must find the person **where** / **who** is making these beautiful shoes," he said.

3 The shoemaker worked hard. He **cut** / **is cutting** the leather for more shoes.

4 But that night the shoemaker and his wife **didn't went** / **didn't go** to bed.

9 **Look at the pictures. One picture is different. How is it different? Tell your teacher.**

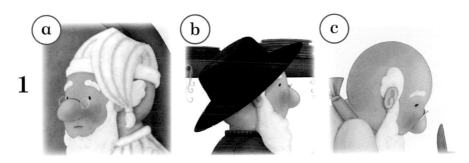

Example:

Picture c is different because the man is not wearing a hat.

10 Read the text and choose the best answer.

The elves worked all night. In the morning, there were four pairs of beautiful shoes. Then, they took their bags and left the shop.

1 The elves were two small men who wore

   a no shoes.   **b** beautiful shoes.

2 The elves enjoyed
   a making clothes.
   b making shoes.

3 The shoemaker and his wife were surprised because
   a they saw the elves.
   b the elves spoke to them.

11 **Look at the picture and read the story. Complete the sentences. You can write one, two, or three words.**

Elves are very small people. We can only see them in stories. Elves often have long ears. They enjoy helping people and animals.

1 Elves ___aren't big___ , they're very small.

2 We meet elves _____ . They don't live on Earth.

3 Elves often have long _____ .

12 Circle the correct picture.

1 Who is as small as a mouse?

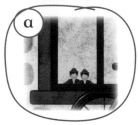

2 Which helps to make shoes?

3 Which thing does the cat want?

4 What did the shoemaker and his wife use for light in dark rooms?

13 **Look at the letters.**
Write the words.

1  v e s l e

<u>e l v e s</u>

2  t h r e l a e

....

3 d l g o

....

4  t u c

....

5  r a i p s

....

14 Write the correct sentences.

This now leather all is the I've got .

1 "This is all the leather I've got now."

make only I can one more shoes pair of .

2 " _____ "

shoes you these Did make ?

3 " _____ "

15 **Read the text and choose the best answer.** 📖 ⭐

1 Why didn't the shoemaker have lots of leather?

a Because he was poor.

b Because he was rich.

2 Did the shoemaker's wife make shoes, too?

a Yes, every day.

b No, she didn't.

3 When did the shoemaker cut the leather?

a He cut the leather at night before bed.

b He cut the leather in the morning.

4 What did the shoemaker do in the morning?

a He went upstairs.

b He came downstairs.

16 Talk to your teacher about the elves, the shoemaker, and his wife. 💬

1 Who helped the shoemaker?

The elves helped the shoemaker.

2 Did they like helping the shoemaker?

3 Did the shoemaker and his wife like helping the elves?

4 Do you like helping your friends?

17 **Ask and answer the questions with a friend.** 💬

1

> How are the elves different from people?

> They are very small and they always wear green clothes.

2 Why were the shoemaker and his wife surprised when they saw the elves?

3 How did the elves change things for the shoemaker and his wife?

4 How did the shoemaker and his wife change things for the elves?

Level 3

978–0–241–25382–3

978–0–241–25383–0

978–0–241–25384–7

978–0–241–25385–4

Now you're ready for Level 4!

Notes
CEFR levels are based on guidelines set out in the Council of Europe's European Framework. Cambridge Young Learners English (YLE) Exams give a reliable indication of a child's progression in learning English.